Karen's Half Birthday

Other books by
Ann M. Martin

Leo the Magnificat
Rachel Parker, Kindergarten Show-off
Eleven Kids, One Summer
Ma and Pa Dracula
Yours Turly, Shirley
Ten Kids, No Pets
With You and Without You
Me and Katie (the Pest)
Stage Fright
Inside Out
Bummer Summer

THE BABY-SITTERS CLUB series
THE BABY-SITTERS CLUB mysteries
THE KIDS IN MS. COLMAN'S CLASS series
BABY-SITTERS LITTLE SISTER series
(see inside book covers for a complete listing)

Little Sister

Karen's Half Birthday

Ann M. Martin

Illustrations by Susan Tang

A
LITTLE **APPLE**
PAPERBACK

SCHOLASTIC INC.
New York Toronto London Auckland Sydney

ISBN 0-590-69186-4

12 11 10 9 8 7 6 5 4 3 2 6 7 8 9/9 0 1/0

Printed in the U.S.A. 40

First Scholastic printing, October 1996

The author gratefully acknowledges
Stephanie Calmenson
for her help
with this book.

Karen's Half Birthday

Freeze Tag

"Freeze!" I called.

I was playing freeze tag on the playground at recess. I tagged my best friend, Nancy Dawes. She froze in her place. I had not tagged my other best friend, Hannie Papadakis, yet. She was on her way to set Nancy free. I caught Hannie just in time.

"Freeze!" I called.

She froze with both arms out in front of her. She looked like a scary monster.

Hannie, Nancy, and I are best friends. We are in the same second-grade class at

Stoneybrook Academy. We play together all the time. That is why we call ourselves the Three Musketeers.

I am Karen Brewer. I have blonde hair, blue eyes, and a bunch of freckles. I wear glasses. I have a blue pair for reading and a pink pair for the rest of the time. I am seven years old. Most of the kids in my class are seven and a half. Some of them are even turning eight.

Speaking of classmates, it was time for me to tag a few more.

"Freeze!" I called again.

This time I tagged my pretend husband, Ricky Torres. (We were married on the playground one day.) He froze in a funny running position.

I was doing a very good job of being "It." I had tagged Natalie Springer when she stopped to pull up her droopy socks; Bobby Gianelli, who used to be a bully sometimes, but is not anymore; Pamela Harding, my best enemy; Pamela's buddies, Jannie Gilbert and Leslie Morris; and Addie Sydney, who is fast in her wheelchair, but not fast enough to beat me!

I heard someone giggling behind me. I reached out and tagged whoever it was. When I turned around I saw Terri Barkan frozen in place. Her twin sister, Tammy, was coming to save her. I ran after Tammy but she got away.

Ding, ding! The school bell rang. Too bad. It was a warm fall day and I liked being outside. Then I remembered that I like being inside, too. That is because I have a gigundoly wonderful teacher named Ms. Colman. She always does interesting things and never shouts or gets angry. Sometimes, when I get too noisy, she has to remind me to use my indoor voice. But she always reminds me gently.

I sat down at my desk and waited to see what Ms. Colman had planned for us. I sit in the front row with Ricky and Natalie. That is because the three of us are glasses wearers and Ms. Colman says we can see better up front. (Ms. Colman is a glasses wearer, too.)

Before I got my glasses, I sat at the back of the room with Hannie and Nancy. Now I turned around and waved to them.

"All right, class, please settle down," said Ms. Colman.

I looked around the room. Everyone looked settled down. Except for me. I was the only one facing the wrong way. I turned to the front of the room and smiled at Ms. Colman. I was ready for the afternoon to begin.

I'm No Baby!

When I got home after school on Wednesday, my little brother, Andrew, was in the kitchen having a snack. Andrew is four going on five. He is in preschool, and he always gets home before me.

"Hi, Karen!" said Andrew with a mouthful of cinnamon toast and cream cheese.

"Hi, honey," said Mommy. "How was school today?"

"It was good," I replied.

"Come wash up and join us," Mommy said.

I washed my hands, then sat down at the table for my snack.

"Do you have any homework?" Mommy asked.

"Nope. None tonight," I replied.

"I do! I have homework," said Andrew proudly. "I have to bring something to school that begins with the letter c."

"That's baby homework," I said.

"It is not! It is real homework and I'm no baby," said Andrew.

He gave me a meanie-mo look. Lately he did not like being the baby in the house. (At the big house our sister, Emily, is the baby so Andrew does not feel so bad.)

"All right, you are not a baby," I said.

I finished my snack in a hurry, then went outside to play with my friends. Andrew was right behind me.

Some kids were already in the tree house in our backyard. The tree house is really cool. My friends and I made it by ourselves. (Well, we had a little help from Seth, my stepfather. He happens to be an excellent carpenter.)

"We are making believe the tree house is a movie theater," said Nancy.

"I am selling the tickets," said Jackie Barton, who is seven.

"I am selling the popcorn and soda," said Kathryn, who is six.

"I want to buy a ticket and popcorn and soda, too!" said Andrew.

"You are too little to go to the movies by yourself," said Jackie. "Little kids need to be accompanied by an adult."

This time Andrew gave Jackie his meanie-mo look.

"Come on, I will take you to the movies," I said.

"No way. I'm no baby!" said Andrew.

He went off to play with Jackie's little sister, Meghan, who is four. She was collecting rocks near the tree house.

Then Bobby Gianelli and his sister, Alicia, showed up. They live down the street. Alicia is Andrew's age and they are friends.

So the big kids went to the movies up in the tree house while the little kids stayed down below.

When we got tired of our make-believe movie, we played freeze tag with the little kids. Nancy was "It" first.

We were still playing when Seth came home from work. He was carrying a bag of groceries. I ran to him and tagged him.

"Freeze!" I said.

He stopped in his tracks.

"You better unfreeze me soon," he said. "Otherwise the ice cream I have in this bag is going to melt. That means no dessert tonight."

"Unfreeze! Unfreeze!" I called.

I tapped him again to unfreeze him. Then my friends and I said good-bye and headed to our houses for supper.

House Switchers

At the little house Andrew is the baby. At the big house he is not. I will tell you how we came to have two houses.

When I was little like Andrew, and when Andrew was even littler than he is now, we lived in one big house with Mommy and Daddy. Then Mommy and Daddy started to fight a lot. They tried their best to get along, but they just could not. So they told Andrew and me that they loved us very much and always would. But they did not want to live with each other anymore. After that they got a divorce.

Mommy moved with Andrew and me to the little house, which is not too far away from the big house in Stoneybrook, Connecticut. Then she met Seth. They got married. That is how Seth became my stepfather. So now at the little house are Andrew, Mommy, Seth, me, and our pets. The pets are Midgie, Seth's dog; Rocky, Seth's cat; Emily Junior, my pet rat; and Bob, Andrew's hermit crab.

Daddy stayed at the big house after the divorce. (It is the house he grew up in.) He met Elizabeth and they got married. So Elizabeth is my stepmother. She has four kids from her first marriage. They are my stepsister and stepbrothers. They are Kristy, who is thirteen and the best stepsister in the whole world; David Michael, who is seven (he is an older seven than me); and Sam and Charlie, who are so old they are in high school.

You already know that Emily Michelle is the baby of the big house. She is two and a half. Daddy and Elizabeth adopted her from a faraway country called Vietnam. I love her a lot. That is why I named my pet rat after her.

Nannie lives at the big house, too. Nannie is Elizabeth's mother. That makes her my stepgrandmother. She came to help take care of Emily. But really she takes care of everyone.

There are lots of pets at the big house, too. They are Shannon, David Michael's big Bernese mountain dog puppy; Boo-Boo, Daddy's cranky old tabby cat; Crystal Light the Second, my goldfish; and Goldfishie, Andrew's pony (ha!). Emily Junior and Bob live at the big house, too, whenever Andrew and I are there.

Andrew and I switch houses every month — one month we live at the little house, the next month at the big house.

I have a special name for us. I call us Andrew Two-Two and Karen Two-Two. (I got that idea when my teacher read a book to our class. It was called *Jacob Two-Two*

Meets the Hooded Fang.) I call us two-twos because we have two of so many things. We have two houses and two families, two mommies and two daddies, two cats and two dogs. We have two sets of clothes and toys and books, one at each house. I have two stuffed cats. Goosie is my little-house cat. Moosie is my big-house cat. And, of course, there are my two best friends — Nancy, who lives next door to the little house and Hannie, who lives across the street and one house down from the big house.

Having two of so many things makes it easier to go back and forth. Big house to little house. Little house to big house. Big to little. Little to big.

It used to get confusing sometimes. But it hardly does anymore. Andrew and I are very good house switchers now.

Teasing

It was Friday morning and Ms. Colman had not arrived yet. The kids in my class were talking about a new TV show they had watched the night before. It was called *Friends and Company*.

"It was so funny when that man, Lucas, walked out of the house in his pajamas," said Addie, giggling.

"They were goofy pajamas, too," said Omar Harris. "They were about three sizes too big on him."

"How about when Lucas's dog tripped him and he landed in the mud puddle!" said Hannie. "I was laughing so hard."

Everyone had something to say about the show. I tried to look interested. I tried to smile when they said funny things. But I had not seen the show. I was not allowed to watch it because it comes on after my bedtime. I felt gigundoly left out. I hoped no one would notice.

"I wonder what will happen next week," said Jannie.

"Hey, Karen, you are awfully quiet," said Pamela. "Didn't you like the show?"

Boo and bullfrogs. Now you know why Pamela is my best enemy.

"I did not see it," I said.

"Why not?" asked Ricky. "It is really good."

"Um . . . our TV broke yesterday," I replied.

"You should have called me," said

Nancy. "You could have watched it at my house."

"Thanks. I will come over next week to watch if the TV is still broken," I said.

I was glad when the kids started talking about something else. I walked to the back of the room with Nancy and Hannie. I wanted to tell my best friends the truth. I knew my secret would be safe with them.

"My TV is not really broken," I whispered. "I was not allowed to watch the show because it comes on after my bedtime."

Just then, I noticed Jannie nearby. About two seconds later, I saw her whispering to Pamela and Leslie. They started to giggle.

"What a baby!" said Pamela loudly enough for everyone to hear.

"Who is a baby?" asked Terri.

"Karen is," replied Pamela. "She could not watch *Friends and Company* because it is on past her eentsy weentsy bedtime."

"Is that for real, Karen?" asked Bobby. "I cannot believe it!"

"Yes, it is for real. Big deal," I said.

"What time do you have to go to sleep?" asked Pamela. "Seven o'clock? Six o'clock? Five o'clock?"

Leslie looked at her watch. "Oops! It is Karen's naptime!" she said.

"Did you bring your baby bottle?" asked Jannie.

"Ha, ha. You are so funny," I said.

"Karen is the class baby! Karen is the class baby!" teased Hank Reubens.

I did not know what to say to Hank because he was right. I am the baby in the class. Some kids were already eight and some would be turning eight soon. The rest of the kids were seven and a half. I was the only one who was just plain seven.

"Good morning, everyone," said Ms. Colman.

Thank goodness. Now everyone would have to go to their seats and be quiet.

I do not like being the youngest one in the class. And I do not like being teased. I felt like crying. But I could not do that. No way. If I did, I knew just what the kids would say. They would say, "Crybaby, crybaby! Put your finger in your eye, baby!"

Karen's Letter

I was still feeling bad when lunchtime came. I sat between Hannie and Nancy way off in a corner of the cafeteria. The Three Musketeers were sticking together. One for all and all for one. That is our motto.

"The kids were mean," said Hannie. "Especially Pamela."

"She thinks she is so funny sometimes," said Nancy.

"Well, I do not think she is one bit funny," I replied.

I could hardly eat my lunch. I was too

upset. I pushed the food around on the plate. (I did manage to eat a cream-filled cookie.)

"Want to play outside?" asked Hannie when we finished lunch.

"I guess," I replied.

I did not really want to go outside. I was afraid the kids would start teasing me again. I followed Hannie and Nancy slowly. I needed to think. By the time I reached the playground I had an idea.

"I'll catch up to you later!" I called.

I walked back to our classroom. I peeked in. Ms. Colman was not there. The room was empty. Good.

I went to the blackboard and picked up a piece of chalk. I stood there for a minute thinking some more. Then I began to write. I wrote and wrote. By the time I was finished, the blackboard was covered. This is what I had written:

DEAR CLASSMATES,

I THINK YOU WERE VERY MEAN TO TEASE ME. TEAS-

ING IS NOT A NICE THING TO DO. IT MAKES THE PERSON YOU ARE TEASING FEEL VERY, VERY BAD. THAT IS HOW I FEEL RIGHT THIS MINUTE. VERY, VERY BAD. SOME OF YOU MAY BE NOTICING RIGHT NOW THAT I AM NOT OUT ON THE PLAYGROUND. THAT IS BECAUSE I FEEL TOO BAD TO HAVE ANY FUN. TEASING IS NOT A NICE THING TO DO. I KNOW I SAID THAT ONCE ALREADY, BUT I AM SAYING IT AGAIN SO YOU DO NOT FORGET. JUST THINK HOW YOU WOULD FEEL IF SOMEONE TEASED YOU. I MAY BE THE YOUNGEST ONE IN THE CLASS BUT THAT DOES NOT MEAN I DO NOT HAVE ANY FEELINGS. I DO. AND MY FEELINGS ARE HURT.

SINCERELY YOURS,
KAREN BREWER

I took a few steps back and read my letter. It was excellent if I did say so myself. And I was pretty sure I had spelled every word right. That is not bad for the class baby.

I put the chalk back and hurried out to the playground. I found Hannie and Nancy at the monkey bars. Just as I got there, the bell rang. It was time to go back inside.

Oh, well. I had missed recess, but I did not mind. I felt much better now that my letter was written.

When we walked into the room, Ms. Colman and the kids noticed the letter right away. (It was hard to miss since it covered the entire blackboard.)

"Everyone take your seats, please," said Ms. Colman. "This letter looks important. I would like to read it out loud."

The kids settled down at their desks to listen. I was feeling a little squirmy myself. I could tell I was blushing, too. My cheeks felt warm. I tried to sit still as Ms. Colman began to read.

"Dear classmates,

"I think you were very mean to tease me. Teasing is not a nice thing to do . . ."

Ms. Colman read every word of my letter. There was not a sound in the room.

Apologies

"Thank you for this letter, Karen. It is not always easy to share our feelings," said Ms. Colman. "Now could somebody tell me why Karen wrote this letter?"

The class told Ms. Colman what had happened that morning.

"I think this would be a good time to talk about teasing and how it can make a person feel," Ms. Colman said. "There is a saying you probably all know. It goes, 'Sticks and stones may break my bones, but names will never hurt me.' Do you think that saying is true?"

My pretend husband, Ricky, was the first to raise his hand.

"Names cannot break your bones or anything. But they can hurt your feelings a lot," he said.

"Yes, they can," Ms. Colman replied. "That is why I am truly disappointed to find out that some of you have been teasing. I thought you were old enough — and kind enough — to know better."

Tammy raised her hand. Ms. Colman called on her.

"I want to apologize to Karen for hurting her feelings. We thought we were being funny, but we were not," said Tammy.

"I apologize, too," said Natalie.

"Me, too," said Hank.

I smiled at the kids who apologized. I thought that was very nice of them.

Just then, we heard a knock at the door. It was Mr. Mackey, the art teacher. I had forgotten all about our afternoon art class. I love art!

"Hello, everyone," said Mr. Mackey. "Am I interrupting anything?"

"We were just having a talk about teasing people," said Ms. Colman.

"Being teased is no fun," said Mr. Mackey. "If you want to have fun, I say make a collage. I have everything you need right here in my cart."

Mr. Mackey is so nice. He wheeled his art cart into the room. It was filled with great stuff — paint, crayons, colored paper, glue, yarn, glitter, and pipe cleaners.

We took turns getting supplies from the cart. I took a little bit of everything, then went back to my desk and got to work. I was in the middle of pasting glitter on my collage when I felt a tap on my shoulder.

I turned around and saw Pamela, Jannie, and Leslie. They were each holding out a paper flower.

"We are sorry we hurt your feelings," said Pamela.

I could hardly believe it. My best enemy was apologizing.

"Thanks," I replied. "The flowers are very pretty."

I went back to work on my collage. The next thing I knew, Natalie was putting a package of smiley face stickers on my desk.

"They are from Addie," she said.

I looked at Addie. She smiled and waved.

Everyone was being so nice. I could tell they were sorry that my feelings had been hurt. By the time I went home I had three paper flowers, a package of stickers, a brand-new eraser, three nice notes, and an invitation from Nancy to have a Lovely Ladies tea party at her house after school.

The morning had started out horribly. But I had one of the best afternoons ever.

A Lovely Ladies Tea Party

Hannie and I each went home after school. We met later on at Nancy's house.

Nancy has a trunk filled with old clothes. They are clothes her mother does not wear anymore, or bought at yard sales just for fun. I put on a lacy pink skirt, a long string of pearls, and a small purple hat with a veil.

"How do I look, dahlinks?" I asked.

"Simply stunning," said Hannie. "What do you think of these shoes on me?"

She was wearing gold high heels that were about ten sizes too big.

"Perfect," I replied.

Nancy was wearing high heels, too. She clip-clopped over to her closet and came back carrying a tea set.

"Hello, tea set!" I said. "I missed you."

It was the first tea set I had ever owned. I had not seen it since Kristy held her toy sale at the big house. (She was raising money to buy new equipment for her softball team, Kristy's Krushers.) I had not wanted to donate my tea set to the sale, but Mommy talked me into it. Then Hannie and Nancy bought it for me as a surprise. Nancy said she would keep it at her house and I could use it whenever I wanted.

We set out the cups and saucers.

"May I pour you some tea?" asked Nancy.

"That would be lovely," I replied.

"Just a half a cup for me," said Hannie.

Nancy poured iced tea into our cups. She held out a plate of oatmeal raisin cookies.

"Cookie?" said Nancy.

"Don't mind if I do," I said. I held out

my pinky like a Lovely Lady and took a cookie from the plate. Then, since I had not eaten much lunch, I took two more.

While we drank our tea and ate our cookies we talked about Halloween, which was not far away.

"What are you going to be this year?" asked Hannie.

"I think I might be a pumpkin," said Nancy.

"I do not know yet," I replied. "I have already been a witch, a ghost, a monster, and Pippi Longstocking. I want to think of something different this year."

"Me, too," said Hannie. "Maybe I will be a black cat."

"I wish we could go trick-or-treating by ourselves," I said. "Without any grown-ups."

"What a cool idea!" said Nancy.

"Do you think our parents would let us?" asked Hannie.

"There is only one way to find out," I said. "Let's go ask them."

We raced downstairs in our Lovely Ladies outfits. While Nancy was asking her mother, Hannie and I took turns calling our homes. Hannie went first.

"My mom wants to speak to your mom," Hannie said to Nancy.

Mrs. Papadakis and Mrs. Dawes talked for a few minutes. Then I called Mommy. She wanted to talk to Nancy's mother, too.

Finally Mrs. Dawes hung up the phone.

"Well, can we? Can we go trick-or-treating by ourselves?" asked Nancy.

"The answer for now is maybe," said Mrs. Dawes. "The grown-ups need more time to talk it over. We will let you know in a few days. I promise."

All right! The Three Musketeers wished the answer had been yes. But maybe was not too bad. At least the answer had not been no. Now all we had to do was wait.

Karen's Good Idea

On Saturday morning, I hopped out of bed and raced to the kitchen.

"Good morning!" I said. "Is there any important Halloween news for me?"

I looked at Mommy. Then at Seth. Then back at Mommy.

"I cannot think of any right now," said Mommy. "How about you, Seth?"

"No. No Halloween news here," Seth replied.

"Are you sure? I thought you might have

something to tell me about trick-or-treating," I said.

"Be patient," said Mommy. "We will have an answer for you soon."

"Right now, how about having some breakfast?" said Seth. "We have cereal, strawberries, and mini-muffins."

"I want everything! I am hungry," said Andrew, racing into the kitchen.

"Me, too," I replied.

I took a blueberry mini-muffin, then poured myself a bowl of Krispy Krunchy cereal. It is my favorite kind. I added strawberries. Yum.

While I ate, I tried a few more times to get an answer from Mommy and Seth about Halloween.

"Is the answer maybe yes, or maybe no?" I asked.

"At the moment, the answer is maybe," said Seth. "How about another muffin?"

"No, thank you," I said. "I am done."

I could see I was not going to get an answer to my Halloween question this morning. So I went back to my room.

I looked at the calendar hanging on my wall. I started counting the days until Halloween. Then I changed my mind and started counting the months to my birthday. When my birthday came I would be eight. I bet if I were eight I could go trick-or-treating without an adult. Eight is very grown-up. No one could call me a baby when I was eight.

"My birthday is a long time away," I said to Goosie.

I studied the calendar some more. My real birthday was a long time away. But wait. My half birthday was soon. It was exactly two weeks away.

"In two weeks, I will be seven and a half like most of the kids in my class," I told Goosie. "I will not be a seven-year-old baby anymore."

Hmm. I was getting an idea. I decided to try it out on Goosie.

"What do you think of this?" I said. "I will give myself a half birthday party. It will be just like a regular birthday party, but everything will be in half. I will serve half a birthday cake. I will invite half the kids in my class. I will ask each guest to bring half a present."

I could tell Goosie thought this was an excellent idea.

I was happy with my idea. And not with just half my idea. I was happy with the whole thing.

May I Have a Party?

On Sunday morning I did not ask Mommy and Seth about Halloween. I tried my best to be patient. That is because I had another favor to ask. I wanted to ask if I could have a half birthday party.

"Good morning!" I said when I walked into the kitchen.

Mommy and Seth said good morning back. Then they looked at me. I could tell they were waiting for me to ask about trick-or-treating. I surprised them. I did not ask.

I sat down at the table and said, "May I have the cereal, please?"

"One box of Krispy Krunchy cereal, coming right up," said Seth.

"Um, Karen? Isn't there something you would like to ask us?" said Mommy.

"No. I am being patient, just like you said," I replied politely.

"We appreciate that," said Seth. "Would you like some strawberries?"

"Sure," I replied. I put a few strawberries on my cereal. I poured in some milk.

I ate my cereal without asking my question. I drank my juice and my milk without asking my question. I popped two more strawberries into my mouth. I still did not ask my question.

When I finished my breakfast, I patted my mouth with my napkin. I pushed my chair from the table. Then my question popped out of my mouth all by itself.

"May I have a half birthday party, please? My half birthday is less than two weeks away. It is a very important occasion," I said.

"Why is that?" asked Seth.

I explained why turning seven and a half meant so much to me.

"All my classmates are seven and a half, or eight. I am the only one who is just plain seven. Sometimes they tease me and treat me like a baby," I said.

"I am sorry to hear that," said Mommy. "It sounds as though your half birthday is very important this year."

"It is very, *very* important," I said.

Mommy and Seth talked it over. Guess what. They said I could have the party.

I ran to my room to tell Goosie the good news and start making plans.

"The first thing I need is a guest list," I said.

I took out a red marker and a piece of paper. At the top, I wrote in big letters: KAREN'S HALF BIRTHDAY PARTY GUEST LIST. Below that I started writing names. I wrote down Hannie and Nancy first.

"Who else should I invite from my class? I can only invite half the kids," I said. "I know. I will invite Ricky because he is my pretend husband. I will invite Bobby because he is a school friend, and a neighbor, too. I will invite Addie because she gave me those smiley stickers. Uh-oh. Pamela, Jannie, and Leslie gave me paper flowers. Does that mean I have to invite them?"

I got an idea. I wrote the names of the rest of the kids in my class on little pieces of paper. I put half the papers in one pile and half in another. I closed my eyes, turned around three times and pointed to a pile.

"Abracadabra! This is the party pile," I said to Goosie.

I added the names of the kids in the party pile to my guest list. I made up a beautiful invitation for each one of them. I decided to hand out the invitations first thing in the morning.

Invitations

I started handing out my invitations as soon as I got to school the next morning.

"Addie, this is for you. Ricky, here is yours. Hi, Hannie, this is for you," I said. (I had already given Nancy and Bobby their invitations on the bus.)

I handed invitations to Omar Harris, Sara Ford, and Jannie.

"Where is my invitation?" asked Pamela.

"And mine?" said Leslie.

"I did not get one either," said Hank.

"I do not have invitations for you," I re-

plied. "The invitations are for my half birthday party. I am only inviting half the kids in our class."

"Why aren't you inviting me?" said Pamela. "I apologized to you and gave you a *handmade* flower. Remember?"

"Me, too," said Leslie.

"I apologized," said Hank.

I did not expect to have so much trouble with the invitations. I tried to explain.

"I did not invite just the kids who apologized to me. I made two piles of papers with names on them. One pile of names got invited and one pile did not," I said.

"I do not think that is very considerate," said Terri.

"It was the only way to do it," I said. "It is a *half* birthday party, so only *half* the class can be invited."

"That sounds like a dumb idea to me," said Tammy.

I gave Tammy a meanie-mo look. I was glad she had not been in my "invited" pile.

"Do we have to get you presents?" asked

Jannie. "You got presents when you turned seven. You will get more presents when you turn eight. Why should you get presents when you turn seven and a half?"

"Because I am having a party, that's why," I replied.

Suddenly it seemed as though *everyone* was mad at me — the kids who were invited and the kids who were not.

"You only have to bring me half a present each," I said.

"Half a present?" said Omar. "How are we supposed to give you half a present?"

I heard someone say I was being a pain. That was not nice. If the person who said it had been invited, I would have uninvited him right away.

All I wanted to do was have a half birthday party.

I did not know why it was turning into such a big problem. I tried to find out who was coming.

"Whoever got an invitation and wants to come to my party, raise your hand," I said.

First a few hands went up. Then a few more. The kids did not look as happy as I had thought they would. I wondered if they really wanted to come to my party. Maybe they were just saying yes because everyone had been mean to me on Friday and now they thought they had to be nice.

Oh, well. The kids who were invited would have fun once the party got started. The other kids would probably forget the whole thing.

No matter what, I was going to have fun at my party. And in less than two weeks, I was going to turn seven and a half!

The Decision

On Wednesday, Hannie and Nancy came to my house for a play date, then stayed for a pizza and salad dinner. When we finished eating, Mommy and Seth had a surprise for us.

"The grown-ups have come to a decision about Halloween," said Mommy. "We have decided that the three of you may go trick-or-treating on your own. There are two conditions."

"Yes!" I shouted.

"What are the conditions?" asked Nancy.

"You must start at four-thirty when it is still light outside. And you must stay on our street," said Seth.

"If you want to go beyond this street, then a grown-up will have to go with you," said Mommy.

The Three Musketeers looked at each other. We were happy.

"Yes!" I shouted again. Then I said, "May we please be excused?"

"Of course," said Seth. "Have fun."

We ran upstairs to my room and closed the door.

"This is so cool!" said Nancy. "Trick-or-treating by ourselves is a big deal."

"I feel more grown-up already," said Hannie.

"Are you still going to be a black cat?" I asked Hannie.

"I am not sure. I might be a leopard instead. I like all those spots," Hannie replied.

"I am not sure I want to be a pumpkin anymore," said Nancy. "I may go as Little

Red Riding Hood. Then I can use my basket for goodies. Do you know what you are going to be?"

"I have not decided yet. Now that we are trick-or-treating by ourselves, I want to be something really special," I said. "Maybe I will go as a royal princess. Or maybe I will be something big and scary like a dragon, or . . ."

Knock, knock.

"Who is it?" I asked. "We are having an important meeting."

"It is me," Andrew replied. "I want to ask you a question."

I let Andrew come in.

"Can I go trick-or-treating with you?" he asked.

"No way. You are too little," I said. "The three of us are going trick-or-treating without any grown-ups. Only big kids like us can do that. You have to go with Mommy or Seth."

"I do not want to go with Mommy or

Seth. I want to go with you," replied Andrew.

"I am sorry, but you cannot come with us."

"I will be good. I promise," said Andrew.

"You will be good if you close the door on your way out," I said. "We have to plan our costumes now."

"I do not like you anymore!" shouted Andrew. "I hope you do not get any treats. I hope you get all tricks!"

He stomped out of the room and slammed the door.

"Little brothers can be pesty sometimes," I said. "Now where were we? Oh, yes. I was deciding what my costume should be."

I had lots more ideas to share with my friends.

Party Plans

When I woke up on Tuesday, I looked at my calendar. My party was going to be on Saturday. That was less than a week away.

"The countdown begins! Four days to party time," I said to Goosie.

I dressed fast and ran downstairs. I needed to talk to Mommy and Seth about my plans. I told them my ideas between bites of cereal.

"My guests only have to get half dressed up," I said. "I am going to dress up my right side and wear play clothes on my left side. I will wear one party sock, one party bow, and one white party glove."

"That sounds like fun," said Mommy.

"We can only decorate half of the living room," I added. "And we should bake half a birthday cake."

"Maybe we should bake the whole cake and serve it half at a time," said Seth. "You cannot ask your friends to bring only half their appetites."

"Why not?" I asked. "They can have a snack before they come."

After breakfast, I rode the bus to school with Nancy. Hannie was already in class when we arrived. I told my friends my party ideas. (I thought about telling them only *half* my ideas, but it was not my half birthday yet. So I told them everything I had thought of so far.)

"So what do you think?" I asked.

Before they had the chance to answer, I got another great party idea.

"How about this?" I said. "We can play

games only halfway. That means there will be no winners or losers."

"And no prizes, either," said Bobby.

He must have overheard me talking. Pamela must have been listening, too.

"I am glad I am not going," she said. "It sounds as though your half birthday party is going to be only half fun."

"You are just sorry you were not invited," I replied.

"You can have my invitation," I heard Jannie whisper.

I noticed some other kids whispering, too. But I could not hear what they were saying. And I did not have time to try to listen. I was too busy making my party plans.

I had *another* great party idea. I would ask the kids to sing only half of "Happy Birthday" to me. And I would blow out only half the candles.

I was having fun already and my party had not even started. This half birthday party was one of my best ideas ever.

Making Costumes

"I have decided to be a dinosaur for Halloween," I said to Hannie and Nancy. "I am going to be an ultrasaurus. That is one of the largest dinosaurs that ever lived!"

The Three Musketeers had called for a special Halloween costume meeting. We were having it at my house on Thursday after school.

"That's a cool idea," said Hannie. "But can you wear such a big costume by yourself?"

"No problem," I said. "I will get someone

to wear it with me. Do *you* want to be the back end of my ultrasaurus?"

"No. I still want to be a leopard," Hannie replied.

"Nancy, do you want to wear my costume with me?" I asked.

"I am sorry, Karen. I still want to be Little Red Riding Hood," Nancy replied.

"But it will be fun to be a dinosaur. Maybe all three of us can wear the costume," I said.

Hannie and Nancy just shook their heads.

Hmm. I did not know who else I could ask to be a dinosaur with me. But I was sure I would find someone. Especially after everyone saw how my costume turned out. All I had to do was make it.

The Three Musketeers got to work. Hannie and Nancy had each brought the supplies they needed.

Hannie was marking up a T-shirt with black and gold spots.

Nancy was wearing a red cape her

mother had let her borrow. She was making paper goodies to carry in her basket for Granny.

I was drawing a dinosaur face on an old pillow case Mommy had given me.

We were going to need grown-up help with our costumes later. But for now we were doing fine on our own.

"Do you think this is enough spots?" asked Hannie.

Nancy and I looked at the T-shirt Hannie was holding up.

"I think you need more," I replied.

"Me, too," said Nancy. "How do I look in my cape?"

"You look like you popped right out of a storybook," said Hannie.

"What about my costume?" I asked. "Did I make my dinosaur face too scary? I do not want little kids to cry."

"I think your dinosaur looks kind of cute," said Hannie.

"Thank you," I replied. *Sniff sniff.* "Do I smell plants in that basket of goodies you are bringing to Granny? Ultrasauruses were plant eaters, you know."

I jumped up and started chasing Nancy around the room.

"Help!" cried Nancy. "An ultrasaurus is after me!"

Getting Ready

"Happy half birthday to me! Happy half birthday to me! Happy half . . ."

I stopped singing the song halfway through. It was Saturday morning. The day of my party. I could hardly wait for my guests to arrive. But first I had things to do. I threw on some old clothes and went downstairs.

"Good morning, half birthday girl," said Seth. "Come have some breakfast."

While we ate we talked about the things that needed to be done. Baking and icing

the cake. Decorating the living room. Filling goody bags. Dressing for the party.

"I should have woken up hours ago," I said. "We have a lot to do!"

I gobbled down my breakfast. Then Mommy and I got to work baking the cake. I had decided on white layer cake with vanilla cream filling, and pink and white icing.

Mommy told me which ingredients to take out. I put eggs, flour, baking powder, salt, vanilla, and sugar on the table. Mommy and I measured and mixed the ingredients together.

"It says in our cookbook that we have to bake the cake for half an hour," said Mommy.

"That is perfect!" I said. "Half an hour for my half birthday cake. I am going to help Seth now."

I raced to the living room. Andrew was already helping to put up decorations. There were streamers and balloons everywhere.

"Wait! The decorations should only be on one half of the room," I said.

"Sorry. We forgot," replied Seth.

The three of us took down the decorations on the left side of the room and put them all up on the right.

Just as we were finishing, the bell on the timer in the kitchen went off. I raced back to join Mommy.

"We can make the icing while the cake is cooling," said Mommy.

We made two bowls of icing. One pink and one white. Mommy let me lick one of the spoons.

"Mmm. Delicious," I said. "Remember, we have to cut the cake in half."

"Are you sure you want to do this?" asked Mommy.

"Yes!" I replied. "Half a cake for my half birthday."

"All right," said Mommy. And she cut the cake right down the middle.

Next on the list were the goody bags. I

filled them halfway with little half-filled boxes of candy.

Then it was time to get dressed. I put on a pink and white striped T-shirt to go with the pink and white icing. I wore a black jumper and maroon party tights. On my left foot I put on a sneaker. On my right foot I put on a black patent party shoe. I made the left side of my hair into a pigtail. I combed the right side of my hair down and put a pink party barrette in it. I found a pair of white gloves in my drawer and put on only the right-hand glove.

"I am ready!" I called.

I ran downstairs to wait for my guests.

Grumpy Guests

The kids started showing up at twelve-thirty. (That is twelve o'clock and *half* an hour.)

Some of them forgot to wear only half party clothes. I suggested that they take some stuff off. But they did not like that idea too much.

"Who wants to play Pin the Tail on the Donkey?" I asked.

Everyone wanted to play. Seth had drawn half a donkey and taped it to the wall. I was blindfolded first because I was the party girl.

Nancy and Hannie turned me around three times, then pointed me in the right direction. I taped the tail onto the donkey. When I took off my blindfold I found out why everyone was laughing.

"You put the tail on his ear!" said Ricky.

Nancy pinned the tail to his nose. Hannie pinned it on his side. When it was Ricky's turn, he missed the donkey altogether.

I waited till half the kids had a turn. Then I called, "Game over!"

"But it was my turn," said Jannie.

"Sorry, we are only playing half games today. Maybe you will have a turn next game," I said.

We had a funny face relay next. The kids split into two teams. Two big pieces of paper were taped to the wall with an outline of a head on each. Each player had to draw one part of a face. Eyes, ears, nose, mouth. The team that finished the face first won.

"On your mark, get set, go!" I said.

I drew the first eye for my team. Omar drew a nose. The next player drew an ear. The next player drew a mouth.

"Time's up!" I called.

"But we did not finish our face yet," said Bobby.

"You know the rules," I said. "Half games only."

We played half of two more games. A few kids seemed grumpy. I heard Sara say she did not want to start another game she could not finish. Ricky wanted to win a prize.

I was happy when Seth came in and said, "It is time for the cake."

He turned out the lights and Mommy carried in half a cake with four candles. (If I had a whole birthday cake, I would have had eight candles — seven and a half and half for good luck.)

My guests started singing as soon as they saw the cake.

"Happy half birthday to you! Happy half birthday to you! Happy . . ."

"Cut!" I called. "You can only sing half the song."

The kids stopped singing and started eating their cake. Mommy brought out ice cream and cookies, too.

"May I have a glass of water?" asked Natalie.

"Only half," I replied.

"Excuse me. Where is your bathroom, please?" said Jannie.

"It is over there," I said. "But, remember, you can only go . . ."

"Do not even say it, Karen Brewer," said Jannie.

She stomped off to the bathroom.

I thought I was making a funny joke. So did Hannie and Nancy.

"I do not think your guests are being good sports," whispered Hannie. "A half birthday party is a cool idea. I am having fun."

"Me, too," said Nancy. "But maybe you

are being a little bit bossy. That could be why some of the kids are grumpy."

I thought Nancy might be right. I promised myself I would try to be less bossy. That way, the rest of my party would be perfect.

Not-So-Goody Bags

After refreshments, it was time for me to open my presents. Yea! Since they were only *half* presents anyway, I decided I could open all of them.

I opened Hannie's present first. She gave me half a pair of striped socks and a card with only half the words written on it.

"I will give you the other sock when you turn eight," she said.

Nancy gave me half a gift certificate to the Unicorn Toy Store and a birthday card that she had cut in half right down the middle.

"We can go to the toy store next week," said Nancy. "We can use the gift certificate as long as we tape it back together."

I could see Hannie and Nancy had fun getting me my presents. That made me like the things they gave me even more. Most of the other kids were grumbling about how hard it had been thinking up half a present.

Grumble, grumble, grumble.

I got half a deck of cards, half a set of jacks, even half a Barbie outfit. I thought the presents were really neat. I did not know what the fuss was about.

"Thank you, everyone. I like all the gifts a lot," I said. (I was trying my best to be nice and not bossy.)

A few kids managed to say, "You're welcome." The rest of the kids were acting like spoilsports. I decided it was time for a game.

"Who wants to play hide-and-seek?" I asked.

"I do!" called Hannie and Nancy together.

No one else even answered.

"Does anyone want to go outside and play in the tree house?" I asked.

"You will probably let us go halfway up, then make us come back down again," said Jannie.

I could see that most of the kids had made up their minds not to have a good time at my party.

We listened to a couple of tapes until it was time for my guests to leave. On the way out, I handed them each a goody bag.

"Thank you for coming," I said. "Here is your goody bag." (I was still trying to be nice.)

Bobby looked into his half-filled bag.

"You should call these not-so-goody bags," he said.

I heard another kid say, "What a rip-off!"

I was glad my half birthday party was over.

Half Day

When I walked into class on Monday, Pamela said, "Good."

"Good what?" I said.

"That is half of good morning," Pamela replied. "That is all you get today."

"Huh?" I said.

"Happy Half," said Omar.

"Happy half what?" I asked.

"Haven't you heard?" said Bobby. "Today is Half Day. It is in honor of your half birthday."

"The birthday you only invited *half* your

friends to celebrate," said Leslie.

"And they only got to play half games and get half goody bags," said Addie.

"And they got bossed around," said Jannie.

Uh-oh. I was in a *whole* lot of trouble with my classmates. Before I had a chance to answer them, Ms. Colman walked in and asked us to take our seats.

After attendance, Ms. Colman said, "We are going to practice writing the script letter S. Leslie, would you please give out paper to everyone?"

Leslie walked around the room handing out paper. When she got to my place, she made a big deal of tearing my piece down the middle.

"This is all you get today. Half," she said.

I felt like telling Ms. Colman what was going on. But then everyone would tease me about being a baby.

I got half of everything all morning. At lunchtime, I wanted to trade sandwiches with Addie. She had cream cheese and

grape jelly — *lots* of grape jelly. I had left-over turkey.

"Want to trade?" I asked.

"Sure," replied Addie.

I handed her my whole sandwich. But I only got halfsies back.

"Happy Half Day," said Addie.

"You can share my sandwich," said Nancy.

"Thanks, but I am not so hungry anyway," I said.

Half Day was getting me down. I only got half a good morning, half a piece of paper, half a sandwich. I knew if I went out to the playground, the kids would only play half a game with me.

"I am not going outside today," I said to Hannie and Nancy. "I will stay here for recess."

"You should not worry about the other kids. We will play with you," said Hannie.

"That is okay. I feel like staying in," I said.

Thank goodness for Hannie and Nancy.

They were the only ones not mad at me.

I knew I owed my classmates an apology. I had made them feel bad even though I had not meant to. An apology would make them feel better. But I wanted to apologize without facing them.

I knew just how to do it.

Karen's Apology

I sneaked back to my classroom. A letter to the class had worked once. Maybe it would work again.

I peeked into the room. The coast was clear. I sat at my desk and took out a piece of paper. I did not want to write the letter on the blackboard yet because I had a plan. It was a gigundoly good plan, too.

When I finished writing my letter on the piece of paper, I reread it. I decided it was an A+ letter.

I was ready to go to the blackboard. I

picked up a piece of chalk and began to write. Since my classmates had declared this Half Day, I wrote only the left half of my letter. It said:

Dear classmates,
I am sorry if I
I did not mean to
I just thought it would be fun
I hope you will forgive
Your
Karen

I checked my letter for spelling errors. Then I waited for my classmates to return from recess.

They walked in one by one and stood in front of the blackboard. I watched them read my half letter.

"Hey, I feel half better already!" said Addie.

"Me, too," said Bobby. "Now I am only half mad at you, Karen."

"Would you like to put the rest of your

letter on the blackboard?" asked Ms. Colman. "I do not know exactly what is going on, but your letter seems to be working."

I went back to the blackboard and finished the letter I had started. It said:

Dear classmates,

I am sorry if I hurt your feelings.

I did not mean to make you mad.

I just thought it would be fun to celebrate my half birthday the way I did.

I hope you will forgive me for not inviting some of you to my party and for being bossy.

Your friend,

Karen Brewer

"Is there anything you would like to say to Karen before we return to our schoolwork?" asked Ms. Colman.

The kids said they forgave me. They thought my letter was really cool, too.

"I say we end Half Day since the day is half over anyway," said Addie. "All in

Dear classmates,
I am sorry if I hurt anyone's feelings.
I did not mean to make you mad.
I just thought it would be fun to celebrate my half birthday the way I did.

I hope you will forgive me for not inviting some of you to my party and for being bossy.

Your friend,
Karen Brewer

favor of ending Half Day, say I!"

"I!" my classmates replied.

I turned to Hannie and Nancy. They gave me the thumbs-up sign. Things were back to normal.

The Dinosaur Solution

It was a rainy Saturday afternoon. I was in my room reading about dinosaurs. I was also trying to solve my dinosaur problem. I still needed someone to be the back end of my dinosaur costume. Halloween was less than a week away.

I decided to give my friends another chance.

I called Nancy first.

"Hi, Nancy," I said when she answered. "I have been thinking about Halloween. Wouldn't it be fun to be in a costume together? My dinosaur costume, for example."

"I guess. But my Little Red Riding Hood costume is all ready," Nancy replied. "I am going to be dressed completely in red. I have a red shirt, red leggings, and I dyed a pair of my old sneakers red, too."

"Oh. Well, it sounds like a great costume," I said.

We decided to play later in the afternoon. Then I called Hannie.

"Hi, Hannie," I said when she answered. "Wouldn't you like to be in a Halloween costume with me?"

Hannie said she had just finished her leopard costume. She had put the tail on and everything.

I told her the costume sounded great. Then I called David Michael at the big house.

"Hi, David Michael," I said. "I am making a dinosaur costume for Halloween. Do you want to be in the costume with me? I need someone to be the back end."

"No way!" replied David Michael. "I am not going to be the back end of a costume even if it is a dinosaur. Anyway, I already have a costume of my own. I am going to be Batman."

Boo and bullfrogs. Now who was I going to ask? I thought about asking some kids from my class. But they had probably planned their costumes already, too.

I went downstairs to have a snack and think some more. While I was munching on an apple, Andrew walked into the kitchen. Hmm.

"Hey, Andrew, do you have a Halloween costume yet?" I asked.

"No. I do not know what to be," Andrew replied.

"Oh, really? You like dinosaurs, don't you? You could be a dinosaur with me. You could be the back end of my costume," I said.

"I love dinosaurs!" said Andrew. "I will be the back end. Then I will get to go trick-or-treating with you!"

I had not thought of that.

"I will have to check with Mommy and Seth. And Hannie and Nancy, too," I said. "Remember, we are going trick-or-treating by ourselves this year. We may not be able to bring a little kid like you along."

"Then who will be the back end of your costume?" asked Andrew.

"I will go ask everyone right away," I replied.

Mommy and Seth and Hannie and Nancy all said it was okay for Andrew to come along.

"See? You needed me," said Andrew. "I guess I'm not such a baby after all."

He was still the baby of the little house. But he was also the solution to my dinosaur problem. Thank you, Andrew.

Trick-or-Treat!

"Come on, Andrew. Climb under," I said. "And try not to let the tail drag."

It was Halloween. The dinosaur costume was ready. Andrew and I had practiced walking around the backyard. Now we were ready to go out into the street.

I had wanted Andrew to be hidden inside the back end of my dinosaur. But Mommy and Seth made me cut a hole for his head. They said it was not safe for him to be walking around without seeing where he was going.

That made us a two-headed ultrasaurus. There was no such thing, of course. But it looked kind of cool.

"I want to get some pictures of you two," said Seth.

"Say 'Trick-or-treat!' " said Mommy.

Andrew and I smiled and said, "Trick-or-treat!"

Click. Seth took our picture. He took a few more as we walked out the door.

"Remember you must stay together on our street," said Mommy.

"And be sure you are back before it gets dark," said Seth.

When we got outside, Hannie's mother was just dropping her off.

"You look like a real cool cat!" I called.

"I like your dinosaur costume, too," said Hannie. "Look. Here comes Little Red Riding Hood."

Nancy was running across the lawn.

We waved to our parents, then headed down the street all by ourselves. On the way, we saw some of our friends.

Bobby and his little sister, Alicia, were with Mr. Gianelli. Kathryn and Willie Barnes were with their parents.

We waved hi to them. So far, we were the only kids on our own. I felt very grown-up.

Ding-dong! We rang another bell.

A couple who had moved in not long ago opened the door.

"Trick-or-treat!" my friends and I called.

"I like your costumes," said the woman. "What kind of dinosaur are you?"

"We are an ultrasaurus," I replied.

"A two-headed one!" said Andrew.

Hannie flipped her long leopard tail.

Nancy looked behind her and said, "I better hurry. The wolf is after me!"

The woman held out a jar of pennies. The man held out a basket of candy. We took some candy for ourselves. Then we each took a few pennies for our goodwill bags. (Ms. Colman was going to send what we collected to a charity for needy children.)

We went from house to house to house.

We stayed on our street. And it was still light out by the time we were ready to head home.

For the first time, I really and truly felt like the grown-up seven-and-a-half-year-old I was. I had gone trick-or-treating alone with my friends and my little brother. We had followed the rules and had not gotten into any trouble.

And that was not all. I had a bag full of candy and plenty of pennies to share.

About the Author

ANN M. MARTIN lives in New York City and loves animals, especially cats. She has two cats of her own, Gussie and Woody.

Other books by Ann M. Martin that you might enjoy are *Stage Fright*; *Me and Katie (the Pest)*; and the books in *The Baby-sitters Club* series.

Ann likes ice cream and *I Love Lucy*. And she has her own little sister, whose name is Jane.

Don't miss #79

KAREN'S BIG FIGHT

I stormed into David Michael's room. "Why did you steal my lunch?" I shrieked. "You embarrassed me in front of my friends!"

"I embarrassed you?"

"And you can not even write correctly." I put my hands on my hips. "Any second grader should be able to spell *banana*."

David Michael put his hands on his hips too. "Any second grader should be able to spell *banana*," he repeated in a high-pitched voice.

"I do not sound like that," I said. I took my hands off my hips.

David Michael took his hands off his hips. "I do not sound like that," he repeated.

"Stop doing that!" I shouted.

"Stop doing that!" he shrieked.

I was so mad.

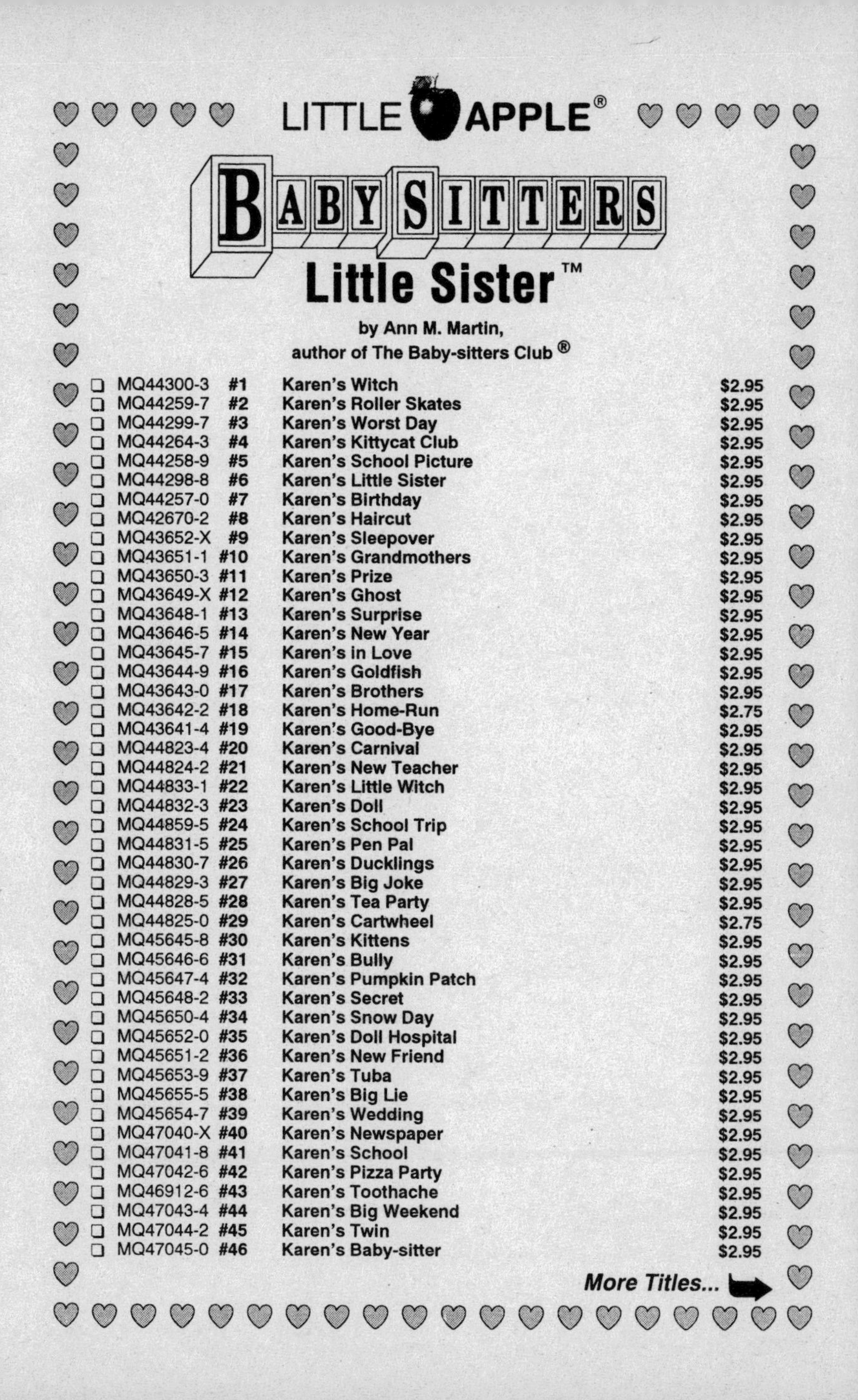

LITTLE APPLE®

BABY SITTERS Little Sister™

by Ann M. Martin,
author of The Baby-sitters Club®

❑	MQ44300-3	#1	Karen's Witch	$2.95
❑	MQ44259-7	#2	Karen's Roller Skates	$2.95
❑	MQ44299-7	#3	Karen's Worst Day	$2.95
❑	MQ44264-3	#4	Karen's Kittycat Club	$2.95
❑	MQ44258-9	#5	Karen's School Picture	$2.95
❑	MQ44298-8	#6	Karen's Little Sister	$2.95
❑	MQ44257-0	#7	Karen's Birthday	$2.95
❑	MQ42670-2	#8	Karen's Haircut	$2.95
❑	MQ43652-X	#9	Karen's Sleepover	$2.95
❑	MQ43651-1	#10	Karen's Grandmothers	$2.95
❑	MQ43650-3	#11	Karen's Prize	$2.95
❑	MQ43649-X	#12	Karen's Ghost	$2.95
❑	MQ43648-1	#13	Karen's Surprise	$2.95
❑	MQ43646-5	#14	Karen's New Year	$2.95
❑	MQ43645-7	#15	Karen's in Love	$2.95
❑	MQ43644-9	#16	Karen's Goldfish	$2.95
❑	MQ43643-0	#17	Karen's Brothers	$2.95
❑	MQ43642-2	#18	Karen's Home-Run	$2.75
❑	MQ43641-4	#19	Karen's Good-Bye	$2.95
❑	MQ44823-4	#20	Karen's Carnival	$2.95
❑	MQ44824-2	#21	Karen's New Teacher	$2.95
❑	MQ44833-1	#22	Karen's Little Witch	$2.95
❑	MQ44832-3	#23	Karen's Doll	$2.95
❑	MQ44859-5	#24	Karen's School Trip	$2.95
❑	MQ44831-5	#25	Karen's Pen Pal	$2.95
❑	MQ44830-7	#26	Karen's Ducklings	$2.95
❑	MQ44829-3	#27	Karen's Big Joke	$2.95
❑	MQ44828-5	#28	Karen's Tea Party	$2.95
❑	MQ44825-0	#29	Karen's Cartwheel	$2.75
❑	MQ45645-8	#30	Karen's Kittens	$2.95
❑	MQ45646-6	#31	Karen's Bully	$2.95
❑	MQ45647-4	#32	Karen's Pumpkin Patch	$2.95
❑	MQ45648-2	#33	Karen's Secret	$2.95
❑	MQ45650-4	#34	Karen's Snow Day	$2.95
❑	MQ45652-0	#35	Karen's Doll Hospital	$2.95
❑	MQ45651-2	#36	Karen's New Friend	$2.95
❑	MQ45653-9	#37	Karen's Tuba	$2.95
❑	MQ45655-5	#38	Karen's Big Lie	$2.95
❑	MQ45654-7	#39	Karen's Wedding	$2.95
❑	MQ47040-X	#40	Karen's Newspaper	$2.95
❑	MQ47041-8	#41	Karen's School	$2.95
❑	MQ47042-6	#42	Karen's Pizza Party	$2.95
❑	MQ46912-6	#43	Karen's Toothache	$2.95
❑	MQ47043-4	#44	Karen's Big Weekend	$2.95
❑	MQ47044-2	#45	Karen's Twin	$2.95
❑	MQ47045-0	#46	Karen's Baby-sitter	$2.95

More Titles... ➡

The Baby-sitters Little Sister titles continued...

❑	MQ46913-4	#47	**Karen's Kite**	**$2.95**
❑	MQ47046-9	#48	**Karen's Two Families**	**$2.95**
❑	MQ47047-7	#49	**Karen's Stepmother**	**$2.95**
❑	MQ47048-5	#50	**Karen's Lucky Penny**	**$2.95**
❑	MQ48229-7	#51	**Karen's Big Top**	**$2.95**
❑	MQ48299-8	#52	**Karen's Mermaid**	**$2.95**
❑	MQ48300-5	#53	**Karen's School Bus**	**$2.95**
❑	MQ48301-3	#54	**Karen's Candy**	**$2.95**
❑	MQ48230-0	#55	**Karen's Magician**	**$2.95**
❑	MQ48302-1	#56	**Karen's Ice Skates**	**$2.95**
❑	MQ48303-X	#57	**Karen's School Mystery**	**$2.95**
❑	MQ48304-8	#58	**Karen's Ski Trip**	**$2.95**
❑	MQ48231-9	#59	**Karen's Leprechaun**	**$2.95**
❑	MQ48305-6	#60	**Karen's Pony**	**$2.95**
❑	MQ48306-4	#61	**Karen's Tattletale**	**$2.95**
❑	MQ48307-2	#62	**Karen's New Bike**	**$2.95**
❑	MQ25996-2	#63	**Karen's Movie**	**$2.95**
❑	MQ25997-0	#64	**Karen's Lemonade Stand**	**$2.95**
❑	MQ25998-9	#65	**Karen's Toys**	**$2.95**
❑	MQ26279-3	#66	**Karen's Monsters**	**$2.95**
❑	MQ26024-3	#67	**Karen's Turkey Day**	**$2.95**
❑	MQ26025-1	#68	**Karen's Angel**	**$2.95**
❑	MQ26193-2	#69	**Karen's Big Sister**	**$2.95**
❑	MQ26280-7	#70	**Karen's Grandad**	**$2.95**
❑	MQ26194-0	#71	**Karen's Island Adventure**	**$2.95**
❑	MQ26195-9	#72	**Karen's New Puppy**	**$2.95**
❑	MQ26301-3	#73	**Karen's Dinosaur**	**$2.95**
❑	MQ26214-9	#74	**Karen's Softball Mystery**	**$2.95**
❑	MQ69183-X	#75	**Karen's County Fair**	**$2.95**
❑	MQ69184-8	#76	**Karen's Magic Garden**	**$2.95**
❑	MQ55407-7		**BSLS Jump Rope Rhymes**	**$5.99**
❑	MQ73914-X		**BSLS Playground Games**	**$5.99**
❑	MQ89735-7		**BSLS Photo Scrapbook Book and Camera Package**	**$9.99**
❑	MQ47677-7		**BSLS School Scrapbook**	**$2.95**
❑	MQ43647-3		**Karen's Wish Super Special #1**	**$3.25**
❑	MQ44834-X		**Karen's Plane Trip Super Special #2**	**$3.25**
❑	MQ44827-7		**Karen's Mystery Super Special #3**	**$3.25**
❑	MQ45644-X		**Karen, Hannie, and Nancy The Three Musketeers Super Special #4**	**$2.95**
❑	MQ45649-0		**Karen's Baby Super Special #5**	**$3.50**
❑	MQ46911-8		**Karen's Campout Super Special #6**	**$3.25**

Available wherever you buy books, or use this order form.

Scholastic Inc., P.O. Box 7502, 2931 E. McCarty Street, Jefferson City, MO 65102

Please send me the books I have checked above. I am enclosing $ ______________
(please add $2.00 to cover shipping and handling). Send check or money order – no cash or C.O.Ds please.

Name ________________________________ Birthdate ______________

Address ____

City ______________________________ State/Zip ______________________

Please allow four to six weeks for delivery. Offer good in U.S.A. only. Sorry, mail orders are not available to residents to Canada. Prices subject to change.

BLS296